ONE BREATH
SECOND WIND
BY JORDAN Z. LOWE

To Mum, Dad, my brothers and sisters, my
nephews and nieces, my loving grandparents, Dr
Robyn Fried, Mrs Theresa Goodwin, Mrs Lynne
Sherwood, Mrs Karen Holmes, my dear friend
Kate, my dear beloved Olivia and all of my friends
who have supported me through writing my stories.

Thank you for inspiring me to share my stories
with the world.

Foreword

Here we are and back again, A Hobbit's Tale by Bilbo Ba- okay, I'm sorry. I had to.

Anyway, this little experiment I finished back in late 2018 ended up being very successful. I've heard people say a lot of good things about One Breath since its release, which made me so happy. Thank you so much!

My original plan was to leave it as a single story. But people (and I) liked it so much, I considered a sequel. But I was lost on what to do for a sequel, apart from giving Kaia another very, very, very deep body of water to dive in.

But then when I was talking with my on-line friends, it hit me. Maybe it was time for Kaia to make a friend. Someone who loved the water just as much as her. Someone willing to dive with her to the bottom of their problems and back...

....I think you know the rest.

And here we are, about to take the plunge once more. Without further ado,

Let's dive in!

Kaia's (and Yuki's) Diving Log

Contents

PREVIOUSLY . . .

Kaia Cayden, a beautiful, gifted young diver in the Hidden Sapphire Archipelago went on her most dangerous dive yet after her parents went missing during an expedition to the Sunken Mazes.

She found out a lot more than she bargained for. Before she knew it, she was in chains. Held captive in a prison run by a legendary species known as the Gilled Ones, in the city of Undala Paradiso. However, she was quickly bailed out by the Gilled One's Prince, Olv.

Thanks to Olv's counsel, Kaia was set free and allowed to gather information on her parent's whereabouts. Olv, curious about humans, gave Kaia a present in the form of a sapphire wristband. She learned where they were through the Gilled One Elder Marnik. He told them they were down in the Dark Catacombs, where a terrifying beast known as the Dark Avarice dwelled.

Hearts full of courage, Kaia and Olv went down alone. Finding a large stone gate blocking their path, they eventually managed to open via keys which they retrieved from a huge octopus that tried to catch Kaia and the Forgotten Banker, a Gilled One who lived trapped in a caved-in vault.

Getting past the gate, Olv and Kaia were beginning to form a bond. But their tender moment was short lived as they were swallowed by the Dark Avarice itself. Using their tools, they managed to escape, only to find the ruined subs used by Kaia's parents...

Olv inspired the despairing Kaia not to give up, as they worked together to kill the Dark Avarice. Afterwards, they found Kaia's parents and their crew, alive and well. Kaia released them towards the surface, Olv carrying her up as she struggled to hold her breath any longer.

When they reached Undala, Olv was forced to let Kaia swim back to the surface on her own, who departed from him with a kiss. Making it to the surface when her lungs were set to burst, she passed out, exhausted but happy...

One year later....

DIVING LOG ENTRY 1

Time until big dive: 3 weeks

In the underwater city of Undala Paradiso, home to the Gilled Ones, a new breath of life sweeps through the streets like a gentle tide. While many residents woke up and set up their shops and prepared their voices, ready to sell their goods for another day, some headed down to what were until recently the Dark Catacombs.

With the Dark Avarice dead and gone, the catacombs were safe to live in again, treasures once thought lost were returned by a Gilled One known as the Forgotten Banker. The city was no longer heavy with fear, no longer in danger of stagnation, all because of two brave young souls...who were currently playing in the coral gardens.

Gliding over the corals, anemones and seafloor flora, the Gilled One's soon to be crown prince, Olv Atlon, was looking around vigilantly for something...or rather, someone. Floating still, he slowly rotated, scanning the gardens. They were virtually empty, save for fish and the odd visitor. Then he spotted something else. Bubbles. Air bubbles.

"I have you now!"

Swimming right for the source of the bubbles, Olv hastily rummaged through the kelp fields, watching for more bubbles.

Just as he thought, there she was. Kaia Cayden. His girlfriend. She lay amongst the kelp, smiling sheepishly, cheeks puffed up with her breath. She then held up her board on which she had written in advance.

You found me! Please, dear prince. Carry me to where I may breathe!

With a happy blush, Olv carried Kaia in a princess-cradle manner, holding her in his arms against his chest and shoulders. As he swam towards their castle, Kaia nuzzled him lovingly, blowing bubbles into his face to tickle him, making him laugh uncontrollably.

"H-hey! Stop that! That tickles!"

Kaia kept blowing bubbles, nuzzling his cheeks with her puffy cheek. Olv put a playful stop to it by clamping her lips and nose shut.

"Now, now, Kaia. You need that air. Now be a good girl and hold it in, okaaaay?"

Kaia pouted and nodded, going back to just hugging him. Passing the streets, the pair glide inside the massive limestone castle. The castle itself was huge, as tall as the rock ceiling above the city and built into the rock itself. There was no sturdier structure. Inside was lit with beautiful sea lanterns, and not a single impurity or barnacle was in sight. Up the stairs they went to Olv's bedroom; a cosy little bedroom with three large shelves for scrolls and books, a large chest containing his childhood toys, and a large clam shell bed.

But there was also a new addition to the room: a large, suspended, bell-shaped dome hanging from the ceiling with an air pocket inside of it. This was recently built by order of Olv, so Kaia had somewhere to breathe. Olv lifted her up into the pocket, letting her refill her lungs with a mild puff.

"My hero!"
She giggled, wrapping her arms around him.

"I must say, Kaia. You have a habit of hiding in the darnedest of places. Remember our first game of hide and seek? You hid in the bottom of my toy chest for 3 hours, even managing to lock yourself in! I still have no idea how you managed that."

Kaia laughed again, this time scratching the back of her head in embarrassment.

"Eheheheh...sorry, I do get a bit ahead of myself when I'm in the water. I guess I've gotten a bit bolder since meeting you. With you, I feel like I can do anything."

Olv gently put his hand on Kaia's cheek.

"That's what worries me. I kind of get scared you might push yourself too hard and end up...drowning. You put on a brave face that time, but I could tell you were set to burst. You were already turning blue, for goodness sake. I just want you to know your limits. Please?"

Olv looked her in the eye with genuine concern and caring for her. How could Kaia say no to that?

"Okay. I'll try to ease up for you. I don't want to drown either."

She smiled, kissing him gently on the lips. Sharing a long, loving embrace, their moment was shattered by Kaia's watch beeping.

"Aww, dang it. Gotta go home already? Man, time flies when you're having fun."

Olv was sad to let her go, but knew he had to.

"Thank you for coming, Kaia. Be safe on the journey home, ok?"

Kaia nodded, resetting her watch.

"I love you, Kaia."

Blushing, Kaia giggled and kissed him one last time. "I

love you too, my fishy prince."

Holding her breath once more, she dove down and out of the palace, waving goodbye to her boyfriend as she made her way back to the surface. Going back through that cave, she remembered the end of that last dive, how her lungs were screaming for air, but she couldn't stop to rest her arms and legs. It was not a pleasant experience for her. Recalling that, she silently acknowledged that Olv had a point and that she would be more careful from now on.

Finally surfacing, she paddled over to a small, pink mini-jet-ski, her transport between Undala and Ark Epsilon, a gift from her parents and as thanks to Olv. She quickly hopped on and started up the small rotary engine, speeding back home before it got dark.

As the sun slowly went down, Kaia finally arrived back at the artificial island, parking her jet ski next to a complex of floating homes, switching on its electronic lock, so no-one could steal it. She trudged onto the wooden dock, her footsteps splashing seawater on the dock's floor panels. She weaved through the odd group of people on her way back to her house, which was a cosy yet spacious chestnut beach house conveniently close to the ocean, yet had emergency enclosure barriers ready to deploy in case of tsunamis and flooding.

Brushing herself dry with a towel, Kaia flopped onto the soft couch next to her parents, Victor and Lia who were also winding down for the day. Lia patted Kaia's forehead gently with a smile.

"Welcome back, my little sea gem. How was your little play date? Was Prince Olv good to you today?"

Kaia nodded with the biggest grin while looking over backwards at her mother. She blushed thinking of her beloved.

"Yeah, we had so fun. We always do! He's just so cute when I get him all flustered with my "mermaid-like" charms, as he described them."

She quipped that last part in jest, laughing cheekily. Lia giggled in return.

"Well, we must surely visit them sometime, when we can find a break in work, right my little Viking?"

She turned to Victor, who broke his gaze from his tablet, nodded hastily, with a sheepish laugh.

"Ah, yes, yes. We surely must, as I am VERY eager to build relations with the Gilled Ones. They are one of the Hidden Sapphire's greatest legends, after all."

He then turned to Kaia, who tilted her head at him.

"Now, Kaia, some new families are arriving to the island tomorrow. I want you to try and make friends with some of them. I know you like the Gilled Ones, but you need friends on land too, okay?"

Kaia couldn't argue with that. She wasn't against making friends. She was happy if she found someone to swim with. She nodded in agreement.

"Good girl. Now go wash up for dinner."

"Kaaaay."

Kaia hopped up, carrying on with the rest of her evening. She slept like a baby that night, dreaming of her dear Olv.

DIVING LOG ENTRY 2

Time until big dive: 3 weeks

Kaia woke up bright and early, getting ready with her family to welcome Ark Epsilon's new arrivals, though she didn't like wearing an electric blue formal dress too much. She was far more comfortable in her black and white wetsuit. But she chose to bear it for the time being as they waited at the island's international airport, located on the massive flat roof of the artificial structure.

Just as everyone legs were getting sore from standing around in the terminal, a large passenger plane touched down right on time. Its passengers were excited yet weary from the flight. There was quite a gathering of families; some from Europe, some from America, some from Australia and some from Asia, among others. The locals welcomed the new arrivals with kind greetings and salutations while the kids greeted each other despite their language barriers.

Though Kaia didn't want to disturb or butt into anyone else's conversations, she needed to make a good impression. So she looked around, spotting the last family to leave the plane. A Japanese family of three, a scruffy and tired black-haired mother and father and their daughter with fluffy greyish brown hair... and in a wheelchair. Kaia looked at the daughter and saw her legs were merely stubs, no knees, no feet, barely even thighs.

Kaia felt bad for the girl, seeing everyone else was preoccupied except for her. So, she approached the family with a gentle wave.

"Hi there! I'm Kaia. Kaia Cayden. Welcome to the Hidden Sapphire. What are your names?"

The daughter looked at her, downcast, her eyes hidden by her hair.

"...Yuki. Yuki Ruki. Umm...sorry. I don't wanna talk right now. I'm tired. Maybe later?"

Kaia felt a bit bad for disturbing her, worrying she may have come across badly.

"Oh, um, okay. I'll be down at the family ports, if you wanna talk!"

She awkwardly waved to them as they left without a word, clearly eager to get to their new home and rest.

"...Must have been a long flight."

After the welcomes were finished, the new families moved into their new abodes. Kaia and the other families gathered for lunch at the family ports, a long waterfront market with a wide variety of delicious foods, perfect for special occasions.

Kaia waited, dipping her toes into the water, looking worried that she had hurt Yuki's feelings. Looking she saw Yuki's family finally rocking up to the party, looking fresher than they were before. Dressed in a black shirt and white shorts, she wheeled up to Kaia, keeping her distance from the water. She waved more gently now, being delicate with the new arrival.

"Hi Yuki! Are you feeling better?"

"...A little. Needed a shower and a nap. Sorry if I offended you before. I was extremely tired."

Kaia shook her head.

"Oh no, not at all. I'm fine. So...can we tell each other about ourselves formally?"

Yuki nodded.

"You first."

Kaia nodded, clearing her throat.

"My name is Kaia Cayden. I'm 14 this year. I LOVE swimming. So much I spend more time in the water than on land. I have a boyfriend named Olv, who is a Gilled One and an absolute cinnamon roll at that!"

Yuki tilted her head at Kaia's gushing.

"What? The heck is a Gilled One?"

"Oh, you don't know? They're an ancient race in the Hidden Sapphire, water-breathers living in a deep-sea city called Undala Paradiso. He even gifted me this beautiful sapphire bracelet."

As Kaia showed her sapphire from Olv to Yuki, Yuki was even more confused.

"Wait, if your boyfriend is a water-breather, does that mean you have to bring scuba gear on every date?"

Kaia snickered.

"Scuba? Pffft! I don't need scuba gear! It only slows me down."

"Then...how do you spend time with him??" Kaia

looked at the ocean with a confident glint.

"I hold my breath, silly. I can hold my breath for several hours, which he loves."

Yuki stared at Kaia in disbelief.

"Nuh-uh. You're fibbing. I can barely manage half an hour."

Kaia's eyes widened in surprise and excitement.

"You have a long breath hold too?! OMG, I thought I was the only one! You like to.... swim?"

She stopped mid-sentence, looking at Yuki's stubs. She covered her mouth, realising how insensitive that sounded.

"...I can barely swim now...I used to be a surfer...but then... a shark bit my legs. They had to be amputated."

Kaia covered her mouth in shock.

"I..I'm so sorry."

Yuki shook her head. .

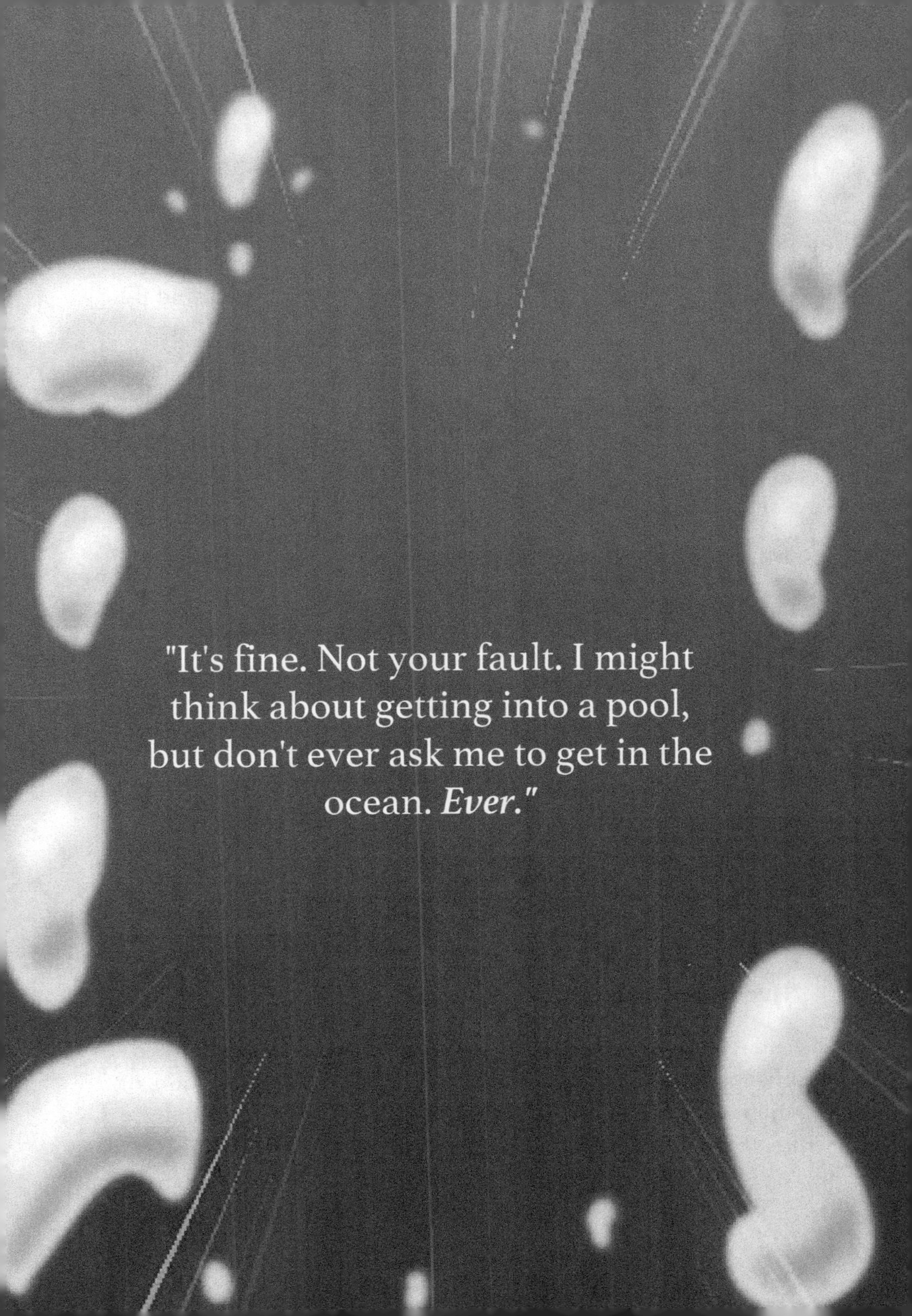
"It's fine. Not your fault. I might think about getting into a pool, but don't ever ask me to get in the ocean. *Ever.*"

Kaia understood completely, clear as day. She bowed in apology.

"Well, we can stay out of the water for now. Do you mind if I visit you?"

Yuki nodded.

"I wouldn't mind. My parents have been nagging me to make friends, anyway."

Kaia sighed.

"Mine too. They say I spend too much time out there."

Yuki laughed a little.

"I'm surprised they LET you out there."

Kaia scratched the back of her head.

"Well, it's a long story, but I'll tell it when I visit."

Yuki's parents called for her to come back, meaning it was time to go.

"Sorry, Kaia. Gotta go. Maybe you can come at 4?"

Kaia nodded with enthusiasm.

"Heck yeah! Looking forward to it!"

And true to her word, Kaia changed back to her wetsuit and strolled over to Yuki's new home, located on the upper floors of the main island. The halls and walls were crisp and clean white, the very air free of impurity or odour. The top levels were illuminated naturally by the sun, a glass skylight above letting the sunshine through. Kaia didn't mind the synthetic feel, but she always preferred the natural deep blue of the ocean. Standing at the front door labelled "Ruki", Kaia gently knocked. Yuki's mother answered the door, still looking a bit weary from before.

"Oh? Are you that Kaia girl? Please, come in. Yuki's been excited to see you."

Inviting her inside, she brought the visitor into a cosy, but not cramped, six room establishment, still a bit messy from unpacking.

"She's in the window room, at the end of the hall. She's already finished her unpacking."

Kaia nodded, bowing in gratitude to Yuki's parents before heading into her room. The room was very dark in lighting, except for a blue light from her computer screen, Yuki furiously typing away. It seemed she was playing an online multiplayer game. One that required a lot of concentration. As the apex of the battle was quickly looming chaos reigned on the field. But Yuki demonstrated exceptional skill in this game, felling the enemy team with minimal effort.

"Wow."

That's all Kaia could say. Yuki turned to see her, surprised.

"Hey, Kaia. Sorry, I didn't hear you come in. So, uh...welcome, I guess."

Kaia smiled and nodded.

"Thank you. So, you play a lot of video games, I take it?"

Yuki nodded.

"My dream is to be a game designer one day. I want to make lots of video games that people can enjoy. Especially water-related games, because there are WAY too few of those these days. But..."

Yuki then looked downcast; Kaia leaned forward with worry.

"But?"

Yuki's hands tensed up, shaking lightly.

"I'm still terrified of deep water, even in video games. I'm scared of what it can do, what it contains. Heck, even drowning scares me stiff. And yet you've claimed to have dived to the bottom of the ocean and back on one breath without batting an eyelash. I'll be honest, I still don't believe you."

Kaia furrowed her brow.

"It wasn't easy, I can say that. I would even admit if I was under a minute longer than I was, I would have drowned. But I can prove it to you, if you want. I'll hold my breath for the whole time I'm here. Sound fair?"

"You're on. My record is about 32 minutes. You can beat an hour, I'll believe you. I'll even try to swim with you."

Kaia nodded with a determined brow, taking the biggest breath and holding it, puffing up her cheeks. As an extra measure, she took some clips from Yuki's desk and clipped her nose shut. Yuki took that as a challenge, holding her breath as well, puffing her cheeks up bigger than Kaia's.

Locking eyes, they stared each other down in a battle of silent endurance, not making a sound, not making a move...until they got bored. Yuki pointed to the assortment of manga she had sorted, motioning that Kaia could read one if she wished. She did, taking out the first volume of a well-known title, whilst Yuki pulled out a handheld game console with detachable hand controllers, both of them still holding their breath.

Having something to do, the minutes ticked by. By the time Kaia was halfway through her manga, Yuki's face was starting to turn red, as she started to have trouble concentrating. But she shrugged it off, continuing with her game. A few minutes, later her chest was starting to burn. A few minutes after that, she put her game down, holding her throat.

Verging on 30 minutes now, Yuki was really struggling, her cheeks turning light blue and her face sweating, while Kaia hadn't even broken a sweat. Her cheeks were bulging now with stale air, holding her mouth as her face now turned deep blue, darkness forming in the corners of her eyes.

Struggling
Totally Chill

Then, as her nose clips were pretty much ready to shoot off....she could take no more. She took off her clips, taking an explosive breath as colour returned to her face, while Kaia was still holding strong.

"H.... how....do.... you....do that...?"

Yuki asked in between ragged gasps, catching her breath in a hurry.

"Well...you can't last an...an hour, right? No...no way."

Yuki flopped backwards on her chair, admitting defeat. Not wanting to dwell on it, she got back to her game and Kaia back to reading. The minutes ticked by...with an hour passing without them realizing. When Kaia was done with her book, she checked her watch. She'd been holding for an hour and twenty minutes, and her cheeks weren't even sore! Yuki noticed as well, her jaw dropping in disbelief.

"Well, shoot. Guess you are the real deal. Honestly, I'm a bit jealous."

Kaia took her clips off, catching her breath. She got up from her chair, patting Yuki's head.

"You're honestly really strong. Wanting to face water again after such a horrible accident, that takes a lot of guts."

Yuki's lip quivered.

"That's the thing. I'm too scared to do it on my own. Scared that my arms aren't enough to keep me afloat."

Kaia stood up proudly, puffing her chest.

"Well, you won't have to do it alone. I'll swim with you and make sure you have a good time and learn to love the water again! The water is scary, yes. But it's also beautiful and full of life. I'll be happy to share that with anyone, especially those who can match my lungs."

Yuki's face lit up with hope. She was almost moved to tears.

"Thanks...thanks so much. When can we start? I'm ready!"

"Public pool on 6th level. 9am sharp. See ya there, Yuki!"

She said with a wink as she waved at the door, Yuki waving back as she departed with a skip in her step. Yuki's mother came into Yuki's room and saw her daughter crying.

"What's wrong, Yuki? Did she hurt you?" Yuki

shook her head, wiping away her tears.

"I'm just happy."

DIVING LOG ENTRY 3

Time until big dive: 19 days

The pool where Kaia was waiting was quiet in the early morning save for a few earlier risers practicing their laps. Kaia dipped her feet in the water, the smell of chlorine in her nostrils. Right on time, Yuki rolled up to her, blue and white sports bag in hand.

"Hey Yuki! You excited?"

Yuki was sweating slightly being so close to the deep end in her wheelchair.

"Well, yeah, but actually no."

Kaia stood up and held her hand.

"It'll be okay. I'll be here the whole time."

A quick change later, Kaia and Yuki were ready to go, Kaia in her black and white wetsuit, Yuki in a black rash guard and grey swim shorts. They started at the shallows, Yuki getting off her wheelchair and hoisting herself onto the stairs. Kaia was right beside her as they slowly waded into deeper waters.

When they got to Yuki's shoulder depth, she stopped, her stubs barely touching the bottom. Yuki started to paddle her arms in rhythm, to practice keeping herself afloat. She even tried kicking for extra buoyancy. Heading a just little deeper, Yuki was managing to keep her head above water, Kaia watching right beside her.

Then, Yuki turned around and paddled back to shallower waters as she was already getting tired. She caught her breath, hanging onto the poolside.

"Sorry...it's...its been a while."

Kaia patted Yuki's back in encouragement. "It's

okay. We'll go again when you're ready."

So, they did. Yuki practiced on the shallow end of the pool, getting a little further with each attempt until she could do no more for the day. So, they made it a daily routine whenever they could. Each day, Yuki got further and further before Kaia had to help her, her stamina getting better with each try, Yuki getting braver with each try.

A whole week passed before she finally did it; making it from one side of the pool to the other. That moment as she got closer to her goal, her arms on fire as she gave it everything she had despite her disability, and that sweet, satisfying feeling of the wet marble on her hands as she held the pool's edge. Kaia hugged her in congratulations.

"You did it, Yuki! You're so awesome!"

Yuki huffed and puffed with a smile of accomplishment, hugging back in gratitude.

"Haaah...thanks...I couldn't...have.... done it...without you."

Kaia then looked her in the eye, with a serious expression.

"I don't want to rush you...but are you ready to go *under* the water?"

Yuki gulped deeply. This part she was dreading. After all, the dreaded bite happened underwater. But she had to go back eventually. She shakily nodded, taking some deep breaths. Kaia stayed right by Yuki's side, ready to go down with her. With one last breath, she held it and closed her eyes, letting the water pull her down.

The sounds around her muffled and deafened, the sounds of bubbles filling her ears as she opened one eye just a crack.

When she saw Kaia, her eyes opened right up. Her beautiful brown flowing hair, her glistening tanned skin and her warming, puffy-cheeked smile made Yuki feel safe. It was going to be okay, even in the water, where neither of them could even breathe.

Letting loose a few bubbles, Yuki lightly paddled on her own, moving slowly through the water, with Kaia following right beside her. Her swimming was a little lumpy, but she was moving, which was good. But she was not as fast as Kaia, who glided beside her with ease. She twirled around, her hair flowing beautifully through the water.

Yuki could not help but feel jealous. So, she decided to try and catch Kaia while she wasn't looking. She paddled behind Kaia before hugging her from behind, binding her arms with a cheeky smile.

Yuki shot a look at the surprised Kaia that basically said "Showoff." Kaia pouted at Yuki and tried to struggle free. But Yuki's grip was tight. Very tight. Kaia couldn't budge free. She squirmed and struggled, but to no avail.

Yuki then raised a thumb upwards, pointing to the surface. Kaia understood with a grin, kicking off the ground and upwards, Yuki still holding her. Taking light gasps for air, Yuki and Kaia couldn't help but laugh at their little underwater exchange.

"So, Yuki, how was it being back under?"

"Um...it was still scary, to be honest. But...you being there made it a lot easier. Made it sort of... not so scary, ya know? So... thanks."

Kaia smiled, patting Yuki's head softly.

"It's cool, Yuki. I'm glad you're getting used to it again. Though I understand if you want to stay away from the ocean. We can just stay here."

Yuki's hands clenched, water droplets dripping from each strand of hair.

"Umm...give me a couple more days here. Let me get used to being under a bit more. Then maybe...*just* maybe... I might try the dock waters."

Kaia's face lit up.

"Sweet! If you do, you can meet my boyfriend, Olv! Oh, you are going to LOVE him! He's so sweet and kind- "

Yuki shoved a hand over Kaia's mouth, stopping her there.

"Ok, ok. Chill, girl. Give the single ladies a break." Kaia

scratched the back of her head, embarrassed.

"Right, sorry. My bad. Sooo... wanna go under again?"

They did. For another three days they came back to that same pool, allowing Yuki to get used to swimming underwater again. Eventually, she even was able to swim up to the surface by herself, albeit slowly. If worse came to worse, Kaia was there to help her. Yuki even broke her breath hold record by 2 minutes, making her best 34 minutes.

And when they weren't diving, Yuki would show Kaia her huge repertoire of gaming designs and experience, showing all sorts of different games, game concepts and game demos of Yuki's making that were never finished for one reason or another.

Then...after three solid days of underwater training... Yuki was ready to face her greatest fear: the ocean.

DIVING LOG ENTRY 4

Time until big dive: 9 days

The day had finally come. The sun was just over the horizon, it's orange light shimmering over the top of the water as it splashed against the pier. Yuki sat on the edge, Kaia holding her hand beside her as she looked down into the blue.

"You don't have to if you don't want to, Yuki. We can do it another day."

Yuki shook her head.

"I have to do this…. E-even if its flipping terrifying…!"

Yuki's heart felt like it was about to jump out of her chest, as she took deep but uneasy breaths, preparing herself.

"Okay, we drop in on three, Kaia. No ifs, no buts. If we delay any longer, I might have a panic attack!"

Kaia nodded, holding Yuki's hand as she took deep breaths as well. Then at the same time, they both took one last deep breath before sliding off the pier and dropping into the ocean below in a plume of bubbles. Yuki hesitantly opened her eyes and was suddenly overcome with nostalgia.

The pristine blue, sandy waters brought back her memories as a surfer. She glided through and under the waves without a care in the world, floating over beautiful coral reefs and multi-coloured and fish-housing rocks with minimal effort, not even thinking about air.

Those memories truly made her happy. And not a shark in sight, which put her at ease as she settled on the sand, sitting gently against a pier pillar. Kaia swam around the pillar, checking the time and looking lovingly at her sapphire bracelet, as if waiting for something...or someone.

Yuki decided to try something she'd always wanted to do. She took out her handheld gaming console which was in a waterproof casing to protect it from the salty ocean water that would no doubt ruin the electrics inside. She decided to play a game involving running an island village, something nice and calming to help her save her breath.

Unbeknownst to Yuki, there was indeed a third to arrive, gliding low through the corals, his tentacle crown poking out above. Finally coming out into the open, Olv waved happily to the girls, catching Yuki way off guard.

"Whatblt thble hecblck?!" (What the heck?!) Yuki

gurgled in surprise, Olv bowed in greeting. "Hi,

my fair ladies. I hope I am not late."

Kaia shook her head, blushing and giving him a big hug, lovingly nuzzling her cheek against his. He blushed deeply, kissing her cheek in return.

"So, is this Yuki? It is a pleasure to meet you. I am Prince Olv Atlon of Undala Paradiso, home city of the Gilled Ones. And... Kaia's girlfriend."

Yuki tilted in curiosity, floating up to him.

"Oh, that's right. You can't talk underwater. That's okay. I brought an extra board."

Olv then handed Yuki a small board to write on, much like the one he gave Kaia a year ago. Yuki then gave it a go, scrawling a few words quickly.

SO HOW DID YOU TWO MEET, EXACTLY?

"Well, Kaia came to our territory in search of her parents who had passed through. But the royal guard thought her an invader and put her in jail. That's where I met her. I bailed her out shortly afterwards."

Yuki gave a catlike grin.

OOOH, JAILBIRD ROMANCE UNDERWATER? THAT'S A NEW ONE.

Kaia pouted in embarrassment.

"Eheh...Uh, anyway. We went shopping along the way in our grand markets, which is where I got that beautiful bracelet for her. I've seen her wear it ever since. We went together down into the Dark Catacombs, where her parents were last seen at the time. We ran into some obstacles, like the Forgotten Banker who threatened to trap us if we picked the wrong things to take..."

SOUNDS LIKE A TWISTED GAME SHOW.

"Yes...Um...there was a larger than normal octopus that ensnared Kaia and almost had her..."

YEAH, GLAD THAT WORKED OUT, AT LEAST.

"After that, we ran into the Dark Avarice, a massive creature that drove our kind to the brink of ruin. We barely escaped being swallowed whole by it, then we devised a plan to kill it. But before that, Kaia stumbled into the ruins of her parents' subs... she thought for certain they were dead."

Kaia clutched her chest, remembering that moment all too well.

"She wanted to give up. But I made her stay. With renewed hope, we had successfully slain the Avarice."

Yuki burbled in surprise.

WAIT, WHAT?! YOU KILLED A GIANT THING LIKE THAT? HOW?

"The Forgotten Banker gave us explosives which we used to collapse part of the cave on top of the creature. Celebrating our victory, we were lucky enough to find Kaia's parents alive and well, and we helped them to the surface. It was at that point that Kaia was really starting to struggle. I carried her back up to Undala, where we were forced to part. But not before sharing our first kiss."

Kaia blushed deeply, holding her face as she silently squealed.

A FIRST KISS ON THE EDGE OF DROWNING? THAT'S... WEIRDLY ROMANTIC.

"She just barely managed to surface, that same night, I found her home island...and we've been together ever since."

He finished that story as he lovingly nuzzled his girlfriend's cheek, making her giggle, although muffled.

"So, if you do not mind me asking...what is your story, miss Yuki?"

Yuki hesitated for a moment, putting a hand to her chest.

"If you do not wish to, you do not have to. If it is too much, I understand."

Yuki shook her head, slowly writing on her board.

NAME'S YUKI RUKI. I'M FROM OKINAWA AND I USED TO BE A SURFER. KEYWORDS BEING "USED TO". WHILE I WAS OUT ON THE WATER ONE DAY…

Yuki swallowed a bit of air in her cheeks.

A SHARK BIT BOTH OF MY LEGS. REALLY BAD. IF THE LIFEGUARDS HADN'T SEEN ME AND HELPED ME OUT, I WOULD HAVE DROWNED AS WELL AS BEING EATEN.

Kaia and Olv both went pale with fright. Just imagining the attack was enough to make their skin crawl, let alone knowing Yuki went through exactly the same thing.

WHEN THEY GOT ME TO THE HOSPITAL….THEY SAID MY LEGS WERE SO DAMAGED THEY HAD TO BE AMPUTATED. I HADN'T TOUCHED THE WATER SINCE. NOT UNTIL KAIA GOT ME BACK INTO IT.

OTHERWISE, I'VE BEEN STUDYING GAME DESIGN AS A POTENTIAL CAREER WHEN I GROW UP. IT IS MY NEW

DREAM TO CREATING A WHOLE BUNCH OF WATER GAMES.

BUT…

Her hands shook slightly as she continued to hastily write.

THE WATER, EVEN IN GAMES, STILL SCARES ME. PART OF ME WANTS TO LOVE IT AGAIN…BUT THE OTHER PART OF ME IS SO SCARED OF GETTING IN TROUBLE UNDERWATER AGAIN.

I'M NOT SURE WHAT I WANT ANYMORE….

EVEN BEING DOWN HERE IS MAKING ME SO ANXIOUS. IF YOU GUYS WEREN'T HERE, I'D BE FULL ON PANICKING DOWN HERE, SCREAMING MY AIR OUT.

Before Yuki could say any more, Kaia and Olv looked at each other, nodding. Then they swam over to her, giving her a big, warm group hug, making her blush heavily. Yuki looked at Kaia, seeing she had a worried, warm expression. It was as if she was trying to say, "everything is going to be okay."

Yuki couldn't help but smile, accepting the hug and hugging back. She rested her head to the side, her cheek and Kaia's squishing together softly. She felt so warm and fuzzy, even in the cold and soaking ocean. Kaia started to softly pat Yuki's head, the latter doing the same. Olv looked at the two girls and blushed himself, admiring the adorable, wholesome sight before him.

He watched them and he just couldn't help himself. He inched closer ever so slowly and then...

"Boop."

With a mischievous smile, he started poking the girl's puffed cheeks, making them let out bubbles in surprise. He then looked away, trying to act all innocent. They frowned and looked away waiting for him to try again, not at all convinced by his act.

They closed their eyes again.

"Boop."

He poked their cheeks again, but this time they caught him in the act, grabbing his wrists. He smiled nervously with an uneasy laugh.

"Sorry, ladies. I couldn't resist. You... actually look really cute right now."

They both smiled with a muffled "Awww..." behind their lips. They looked at each other, nodding with mischievous grins. Kaia guided Olv's hand to her face, letting him hold one of her cheeks in his hand. Yuki did the same, her cheeks even bigger than Kaia's, making Olv blush as red as a tomato. They both gave a wide grin, bubbles escaping from the corners of their lips before they both gave him a group hug, tackling him into the sand.

It was truly a beautiful moment for Kaia, Olv and Yuki. One they all silently wished could last forever. But alas...humans need air.

"Boop."

Yuki burbled, releasing a burst of bubbles from her mouth before covering it, her face turning a deep shade of red. She pointed upwards, signalling she needs to go up for air. They nodded, taking her by the shoulders and carrying her upwards to the surface. Kaia and Yuki both took deep gasps of needed air, looking at one another. Kaia started to giggle, which made Yuki chuckle, then they all broke out in happy laughter, after all the fun they'd had the in the blue.

"Hey, Kaia. Thanks. Really, I mean it. You too, Olv."

Olv nodded with a small bow.

"It is of no consequence, miss Ruki. We are glad you are feeling better."

Yuki chuckled with a side smile.

"Just Yuki's fine. No need for that honorifics stuff. But yeah... it's weird. I felt I could be honest down there... like there was no shame in anything. To be honest, I missed it so much."

She put a hand on each of their shoulders.

"It's ironic, to be honest. It's only where we can't breathe... where we can be ourselves."

Kaia gave a wide grin.

"Yeah, you might be right. But who gives a carp? We're all bubbly smiles down here in the deep blue - no exceptions!"

She then gasped in pure realization.

"I just got an AMAZING idea! We should start an underwater club! Where we can do whatever the heck we want. It could start with us, then we can invite others who are good at diving like us."

Olv's eyes lit up with excitement.

"That sounds stupendous, Kaia! Surely we must try that!"

Yuki nodded contently.

"That sounds nice. We should try that in the future, if I can get over my fear."

They all nodded in agreement.

"Then its settled! When we help Yuki out, we'll start this together!"

And so, they made the underwater get-together a regular occurrence. Nearly every morning or afternoon they came to the same pier, bringing Yuki along for the dive every time. On days she was feeling brave, she would ask them to take her out further to see the beautiful corals and lively schools of fish. Other days she was more than content to just chill with her new friends under the pier, playing her games for as long as she could hold her breath, while Kaia and Olv shared a loving kiss or two in private.

It was some of the best days of their lives. Where they couldn't even breathe, they could be themselves.

But one day... Yuki stopped coming.

DIVING LOG ENTRY 5

Time until big dive: 4 days

Kaia and Olv waited at the pier 2 days in a row. But Yuki never came. Olv held Kaia's shoulders to comfort his worried partner.

"Perhaps she has taken ill? I'm certain it is no large issue."

Kaia would have loved to believe that. But still, she worried.

"Wait here, I'm gonna go check on her."

Kaia got out of the water, quickly drying herself before heading up to Yuki's residence. She knocked on the door and Yuki's mother answered, as always.

"Oh, Kaia. Good morning! You must be looking for Yuki, yes?"

Kaia nodded.

"Well, you can see her. But she hasn't been feeling well in the last couple of days. Please try to be gentle with her."

Kaia gave her word before heading to Yuki's room, gently knocking on the door.

"Come in..."

Yuki sounded out of sorts with her response as Kaia entered. Yuki was still curled up in her blanket with only a single lamp on in the room. Kaia sat on the bed, worried for her on seeing her in this state.

"Are you okay, Yuki?" She

slowly shook her head.

"Do....do you want to talk about it?"

She merely curled up in her blanket tighter, not giving an answer. Kaia inched over to her, giving her a hug. Yuki hugged Kaia back through her blanket, at last wanting to open up.

"I've been having nightmares."

Yuki's straight answer took Kaia by surprise.

"Nightmares?"

"Of being underwater. But not in a pleasant way. Getting bitten by another shark, being trapped under a pool or in a box whilst clawing for anything close to air, being dragged to the bottom of the ocean by hands or tentacles, never to see the surface again...where no-one can save me..."

Yuki's tired eyes started to tear up.

"They feel so real...I wake up gasping for air, in a puddle of my own sweat. I can't take it! I'm scared, Kaia. I'm really scared... I don't know what to do."

Yuki was really starting to break down, crying on Kaia's shoulder.

"I can't even *breathe* properly sometimes...it feels like...my fear is drowning me!"

Kaia had no idea what to say. She could only hold her friend close, knowing she was in enormous pain... pain that she may have made worse. Kaia sat in silence, rubbing Yuki's back softly to make her feel at least a little better. It felt like they sat there for hours, without even a word.

"Kaia..."

Yuki finally broke the silence.

"I'm not sure when or if I'll ever come back to the water. I'm sorry."

Kaia shook her head.

"I'm sorry for forcing you. It must have been terrifying, and I have no way of understanding that. But I'm here for you, no matter what."

Yuki rested her head on her friend's shoulder, closing her eyes for just a moments respite.

Kaia returned to Olv later that afternoon, who was worried sick from waiting so long.

"Kaia! You were gone for a while. Is miss Yuki OK?"

Kaia sat on the deck, a somber gaze on her face.

"She's been having horrible nightmares about the water. I think we've made it worse with our gatherings."

She sighed deeply, angry with herself. "I

was too darn insensitive!"

It feels like...my fear
is *drowning* me!

Olv didn't know what to say. He had never known their kind gesture would have this dire a consequence. But regardless, he slapped his cheeks, getting his mind together. He took Kaia's hands, a determined look on his face.

"Do not give up, Kaia. Be strong. We will get her through this, one way or another."

Parting from Kaia with a confident kiss that left her very red, Olv returned to Undala Paradiso, hitting the ancient libraries, determined to find answer for Yuki's ailment. For two days he combed the libraries, searching book after book after book, stopping only to sleep and eat.

Finally, on the second night...he found something drastic.

Olv returned to Ark Epsilon, seeing a very worried Kaia waiting on the port, a tired Yuki sitting on her wheelchair beside her. He waved to them both, sporting a heavy book under his arm.

"Good morning, ladies! I am very sorry to keep you waiting. How has Yuki been faring?"

Kaia sombrely shook her head.

"The nightmares have been getting worse. She's gone two nights without sleep. I'm out of ideas, Olv."

Olv hoisted the book onto the deck.

"But I am not. I have one way that may be able to help. But... it is quite dangerous."

Yuki looked at the book with desperate, tired eyes.

"What is it? Show me. At this point, I'll do anything."

Olv paused for a moment, then nodded, opening the book to a specific page.

"Legend tells of a ruin called the Breathless Temple. It is an underwater temple on a deep-sea sand dune not far from Undala. My people stay away from it, for it has two rules: only air breathers can enter, and they may only enter with the air in their lungs.

In the centre of the temple, which can only be reached by braving many dangerous tricks and traps hidden inside, lies a sacred, one-of-a-kind treasure guarded by an ancient machine, a treasure that grants a wish - *any* wish - to one who claims it."

"It is my assumption that this treasure will rid Yuki of her suffocating trauma! There is one issue, however."

They looked at Olv with worry and concern.

"I know where it is. I found it last night. But it is far out there, in the deep ocean. Furthermore, for the treasure to work, Yuki herself must make the wish."

Kaia held her chin.

"So, I go in alone, bring the treasure back to Yuki- "

Yuki then cut Kaia off mid-sentence.

"Or I go with her and make the wish there myself."

Kaia and Olv looked at her with genuine surprise. She gently put a hand on her tired friend's shoulder.

"But your fear of the deep ocean... are you going to be OK out there?"

Yuki shook her head, her lip quivering.

"No, I won't be ok. Not at all. I'm definitely expecting to freak out something fierce. But you know what? I'm so sick of this. I'm sick of letting this stupid, irrational fear control me. Of letting it smother me. I don't care anymore; I have to get rid of it – or drown trying!"

Tears streamed down Yuki's face as her voice cracked, true despair in her words. How could either of them say no to that? Kaia held a hand to her chest, clutching it tightly.

"Ok. Let's do it. But we need to plan this properly. If we're not careful, it could be dangerous...or worse, deadly. I think.... we could get there tomorrow morning, same time. We'll meet up here, I'll take Yuki to the diving point by my jet ski, while Olv leads the way. I'll pack a small air tank for us to make it easier to get to the temple's entrance, then Olv can hold the fort outside until we return."

Olv nodded in agreement.

"Yes! Splendid idea! I will see what knowledge of the temple's interior I can gather before then. Miss Yuki, is this okay with you?"

Yuki paused for a long, long moment, nodding with teary, happy eyes.

"Thank you...thank you so much. You guys...really are the best."

Once again, they hugged, determined to get through what may be their most dangerous trial yet. Kaia stayed over at

Yuki's that night, secretly preparing with her throughout the night.

As the sun rose, so did they. The time had come once again for Kaia to tackle the dangers of the deep. Only this time, she wasn't as alone. This wasn't for herself, but for a friend in need.

DIVING LOG ENTRY 6

Time until big dive: 1 Hour

The sun had risen with not a cloud in the deep blue sky. The ocean was calm and gentle, the water was clear. The diving conditions were perfect. Bang on time they met up, Olv waiting in the water whilst Yuki sat on the port and Kaia was parking her mini jet-ski, ready to take her friend on board.

Yuki slowly hoisted herself off her wheelchair and into the water, taking Kaia's hand to lift herself onto the back of the jet ski, holding tightly around Kaia's abdomen. A small air-tank was strapped to the back of the craft, ready to use, the two girls strapped on shoulder mounted flashlights for the darker waters. The young Sapphire diver then looked back at her friend.

"Ready?"

Yuki nodded, taking a deep breath to calm her shaky nerves. Kaia started the rotary engine, speeding away into the ocean, whilst Olv led the way, swimming at breakneck speed. The waves became slightly bigger once they went further out, but the conditions were still manageable, even for Kaia's little ride. Yuki's heart was pounding as Ark Epsilon, the nearest safe land for dozens of miles, got further and further away, so she hugged Kaia tighter to make herself feel safer.

After what felt like ages travelling in a straight line, Olv signalled Kaia to stop, making her turn off the engine and engage the portable anchor to prevent the ski drifting away.

"Kaia and Yuki, this is the place. Last chance to turn back, I am afraid."

Kaia leapt into the water without hesitation, swimming up to Olv.

"I remember what you said about not pushing myself. I remember it, clear as day. I'll try to be as careful as I can, for both my and Yuki's sakes. Just remember, if worse comes to worse, I might have to share air with her. She can't hold her breath as long as me."

Olv nodded, quietly gulping as he feared for their safety. But this was his idea, so he stuck with it, getting his mind together as Kaia slowly helped Yuki into the water. Splashing right in, Yuki paddled back up, and held onto Kaia tightly. Olv then released the small air tank carrying it in his arms. Kaia looked right into Yuki's eyes.

"Oh, before I forget. I want to give you a little something."

Kaia reached into her side pack on her hip and pulled out a beautiful sapphire, attached to a necklace chain.

"It's a sapphire I got from the Forgotten Banker. I already have my sapphire bracelet from Olv, so I'll give you this for good luck."

Yuki didn't know what to say. She wasn't the biggest fan of jewels, but this one was especially beautiful.

"A-are you sure, Kaia?"

She nodded confidently, putting the necklace around Yuki's neck. Yuki grasped the jewel tight, making a silent vow never to lose it.

"Okay, it's time. Slow, *deeeep* breaths to slow down your heart, because I know you're nervous. Then we take some huge breaths to pack up our lungs. Then we dive. Ready?"

Yuki nodded, taking deep, though shaky breaths. She was struggling to keep calm.

"It's okay. I'm here. Just take it nice and slow. Go at your own pace."

Kaia's presence brought Yuki much relief. If she was alone, she'd be beside herself with fright. Slowly and steadily Yuki's nerves calmed. Her breaths were slower and deeper, in synchronisation with Kaia's. Then in perfect unison, they both took one last, huge breath before plunging straight down underwater.

Turning on their flashlights, they followed Olv downwards, Yuki pinching her nose and popping her ears to equalise the pressure. She released an odd bubble or two from her lips as they both swam even deeper, deeper than Yuki had ever dived before. Before long, they saw it: a massive, pyramid-like structure, surrounded by small stone buildings and algae ridden stone pillars. It dwarfed them in size, as they drew level with its peak. It was as if early Egypt had sunk into the ocean.

Olv led the girls down further, down to the ground level of the temple where a huge stone door lay open, it's interior pitch black and with unseen dangers lurking within...

Olv set down the tank beside the door.

"I am afraid this is as far as I can take you. You must go in on your own. I'll wait here until you get out, so please, take a breath if you need to."

The girls nodded, Kaia taking two deep breaths from the regulator before passing it to Yuki. She took more than a few breaths, steeling herself for the temple. One last big inhale, and she relinquished the regulator back to Olv.

"Please be careful. May Oci Jun be on your side this day."

Kaia nodded, giving Olv one last kiss before setting off with Yuki, who held onto her abdomen as they swam inside, neither looking back....

Inside the temple's entrance was a huge flight of stairs, leading downwards. The girls followed the stairs, finding out firsthand just how dangerous the temple really was. Bones. Human skeletons dotted the lower stairs, strewn about in several different spots on and at the bottom of the stairs. They both knew what these were.

Past divers who met a watery grave instead of a miracle treasure, in this very temple. This would be what awaited these two if they were not careful.

Kaia knew that. She took a moment to make a quick, silent prayer for these losses.

Oci Jun,

Mistress of Currents,

Nurse of Reefs,

Take these flooded souls into your warming bosom, So that they

may know peaceful rest in the infinite blue.

It was the burial rite of the Hidden Sapphire, Kaia's people and their goddess Oci Jun, the "ocean mother." Kaia wasn't the most religious of her people, but she never, ever forgot to respect the dead. Yuki didn't quite understand, but she thought it best to pay her respects as well, clapping her hands together, in the manner of Japanese prayer.

But they had to move on, seeing their first trial at the bottom of the stairs: three massive stone doors each with a conspicuous symbol on them, and a large hole near the bottom. In front of the doors were three large gold coins with the same symbols as the doors: a halo, a gold coin and a skull.

Kaia looked at the doors intently, noticing that this was a riddle, but of what?

"Mm! Mm!"

Yuki then pointed to a small pedestal with faded writing, signalling to Kaia. They both paddled over to it.

"Three forms of treasure lay upon these doors, but only one leads to true fortune. Learn the difference between treasure worth a life…and treasure that costs a life."

Yuki figured it out, taking out her board.

WE HAVE TO MATCH THESE COINS TO THE RIGHT DOORS.

Kaia nodded, picking up the halo coin and taking it to the halo door. Yuki did the same with the Gold coin, carrying it to the gold door. The coins were weighty, but not too much for even the legless Yuki to manage. Slotting those coins in, they carried the bone coin together to its designated slot. They swam backwards waiting for the doors to open.

....

....

....

Nothing.

The girls tilted their heads in question.

WE MUST HAVE GOT IT IN THE WRONG ORDER.

Kaia nodded in agreement, deciding to rack her brain together with Yuki to figure it out.

Let's take our time thinking about this. It'd be wasting air moving them back and forth.

They both held hands to their chins, deep in thought. Yuki was thinking about the riddle in particular. Kaia was racking her brain vigorously.

"Carp, this one's a doozy."

Meanwhile, Yuki stared at the pedestal, then at the doors. She recited the message in her head, trying to find a connection.

"Three forms of treasure...only one...treasure worth a

life...and treasure that costs a life...a life.... treasure.... life..."

Yuki's head clicked in an epiphany. She poked Kaia to get her attention.

I'VE GOT IT! *"TREASURE THAT'S WORTH A LIFE AND TREASURE THAT COSTS A LIFE!"* BONE COIN TO THE GOLD DOOR, HALO COIN TO THE BONE DOOR AND GOLD COIN TO THE HALO DOOR!

Are you sure, Yuki?

Yuki nodded with surety. She was dead certain that this was the way. So, they removed the coins, shuffling them around in Yuki's suggested order. Once relocated, they slotted all the coins into their slots. Swimming back, they once again waited.

This time, something happened. The doors flashed with light three times, the coins sliding further into the doors. Then a deep rumble shook the whole room as the halo door slid open...whilst the other two fell and shattered into a thousand pieces with a thunderous crash.

Even Olv felt it outside, looking inside to check on the girls.

"HEY! ARE YOU TWO OK?! THAT WAS REALLY LOUD! FLASH YOUR LIGHTS IF YOU'RE OK!"

The girls flashed their lights at Olv, signalling that they were unharmed. Olv sighed deeply in relief as they carefully swam towards the halo door, still shaken by what just happened.

GOOD THING WE STOOD BACK.

Kaia shakily nodded. Swimming into the halo door, they saw a long brick hallway, lit up with bright violet sea lanterns. It was arrow-straight, with a single exit at the end. It looked quite simple... In fact, a little TOO simple. They glided forward, suspicious and ready for anything.

Halfway through the hall, their suspicions were confirmed. Another deep rumble, this time right behind them!

They looked behind to see a massive boulder rolling down towards them, easily big enough to flatten them both. They both swam like they never swum before, adrenaline kicking in hard. Yuki was barely managing to outswim the boulder, both of them darting towards the exit with everything they had as
the boulder got closer and closer and closer....!

They bolted right through the exit, the boulder stopped right behind them. They floated limp in the water, giving their limbs a rest in the underwater equivalent of catching their breath. Yuki's necklace jingled in the current. Needless to say, that encounter cost them quite a bit of air, Yuki's chest already felt the slightest bit tight as she exhaled a small bit of stale air.

Regaining their strength, they swam onwards, seeing a much smaller room than the last one, but there was a major difference: there were wires scattered everywhere from wall to wall, floor to ceiling. Kaia lightly tugged the wires, and it sent the ceiling crashing down in front of them before slowly rising again and resetting, giving the girls quite a fright. Kaia scribbled on her board quickly.

Okay, so no problem. All we have to do is be REALLY, REALLY careful and REALLY, REALLY slow going through this. We'll need to go one at a time.

Yuki didn't argue with that. Despite her fears, she knew going both at once could be fatal. Kaia elected to go first, swimming very slowly and with minimal movement. She had to keep her head on a swivel, for a tripwire could snag on any of her blind spots and that would be the end of it. It was in the middle of this deadly puzzle she began to fully, undoubtably understand the danger of where she was... and what she was doing. It took her several minutes just to navigate each cluster of wires, but eventually, she made it to the other side.

Now, it was Yuki's turn.

Gulping in nervousness, she slowly inched forward, taking it one stroke at a time. Some would think that her having no legs gave her an advantage, for she had more room to work with. But she also found it harder to control, needing to adjust her position and angle more than Kaia did. Her long arms and short stubs stroked in unison, making her look like a swimming jellyfish from Kaia's point of view.

Yuki exhaled a large bubble of air, her chest slightly heaving, making her stubs kick back...and into a wire.

"...Oh snap."

Both girls went into full-on panic in that instant, Yuki swimming at full speed towards Kaia, who grabbed her hands and pulled her back with all her might as the ceiling came crashing down.... Right where Yuki's legs would have been.

Seeing where the stone came down, both were wide-eyed.

GEEZ, GUESS I KINDA DODGED A BULLET THERE, HUH? I ALMOST ENDED UP LIKE A HALF EMPTY ROLL OF TOOTHPASTE!

Kaia had nothing to add to the situation, she was simply glad Yuki was okay. Both of them floated onwards, eager to get far, far away from this room.

Yuki gurgled involuntarily, letting out more air as her face turned a deep red. She moaned in her throat, really starting to worry as she pointed to her lips.

Kaia held her shoulders and gently hugged her, helping her calm down.

Keep holding it in, Yuki. You're a brave girl. You can last a little longer.

Yuki was hesitant, but eventually nodded, patting her aching chest and giving a thumbs up.

It wasn't long before they came to two different paths. One leading upwards, one leading downwards. They had no idea which to pick.

Kaia scribbled on her board.

I'll check out the left path. You check out the right one.

Yuki nodded, carefully floating over the first step.

Suddenly, a loud rumble and crack echoed above them, sending debris raining down behind Yuki - cutting her off from Kaia. She frantically peeked through a hole in the rubble and saw Kaia was okay. But they were now totally separated.

Go on ahead, Yuki! We'll regroup ahead somewhere!

Yuki shakily nodded, being forced to go ahead as Kaia went up the other path. This time, she was all alone. She would have been stumbling in the dark were it not for her flashlight. But the flashlight was her only source of comfort as the spiral path leading downwards got tighter and tighter until she was forced to crawl.

She shuffled her body across the rough, uneven stone, the pressure in her chest growing worse, her cheeks turning redder as more stale air forced itself out through her lips and nose. She wasn't denying it any longer. She needed to move. Fast.

Yuki could at last see light at the end of the tight tunnel. It finally emerged into a cavern-like enclosure, the walls layered with algae with the odd fish swimming in and out through the tiny cracks. And one other thing she was not expecting:

A young boy, appearing around the same age as Yuki, was sleeping gently on the sandy bottom. But this was no ordinary human boy, nor was he a Gilled One like Olv. Yuki quietly swam to get a closer look.

He was different, in an entirely unseen form. His skin was light blue with wavy patterns slowly flowing, much like an octopuses' camouflage. He had the same build as Olv, but his legs were longer, his arms looked stronger and he had fins instead of feet; his hands looked very grippy, each fingertip pointed like a tentacle. He had very smooth, white shoulder length hair, his face peaceful as he slept.

She inspected the boy closely, genuinely curious. She'd never heard of this type of oceanic humanoid. This was even outside the Gilled One's knowledge, as far as she knew. Looking at the boy, she found him fascinating. She thought to herself.

"Whoa, this guy is new. And...kinda cute looking too."

Yuki blushed a little in addition to being low on air, an issue she was reminded of by another reflex from her lungs, as she coughed up more stale air loudly. That made the boy twitch, enough for him to slowly wake up. Yuki bolted behind the nearest rock she was able to reach.

"Whoa! That was too close! I He might look cute, but I have no idea what he's like! He might try to eat me for all I know!"

Covering her mouth, she looked around the cavern for a way out. She saw a similar sized hole as the one by which she had entered and it was leading in the same direction as Kaia. But there was one problem.

"He's between me and that exit! I've got to get there without him seeing me. And I have to do it quick, kinda running on low here...!"

The boy stretched his arms and legs, having fully woken up. He started to lazily swim around, not having much to do in there, whilst Yuki stood absolutely still. Whenever he looked the other way, Yuki would swim from one hiding spot to the next, clutching her necklace so it wouldn't give her away.

But as he lazily glided around the water, he noticed a small stub duck behind a rock in a split second. Curious, he swam closer. Meanwhile, Yuki was scanning the waters to see where he was, but she couldn't see him.

"Wait, where is he? Ah, shoot..."

She turned around to check behind her...

And there he was. Right in front of her. They locked eyes for a moment, before it clicked for both of them. The boy gave a huge, happy smile.

Yuki let out a short, gurgling shriek, spooking the boy back around the rock. In her mind, it was now or never. She bolted as fast as she could towards the exit, thinking the boy was a threat. The boy glided towards her to try and catch her, but she was just out of his reach, his neck was snagged by a locked chain anchored to the ground. Yuki saw the chain and felt relief.

"Whew! In the clear!"

But as she tried to crawl away, she heard sniffling. Looking back, the boy had curled up into a ball, sniffling and whimpering.

"Is he...crying?"

He was. Breaking down into invisible tears, the boy cried in sadness. This made Yuki feel awful. It seemed she was wrong about him.

"Mmm...what the heck. I can spare a couple of minutes."

Crawling back out of the exit, she swam back towards the boy, tapping his shoulder. He looked up, still looking sad, but surprised she came back. Yuki scribbled on her board.

SORRY ABOUT THAT. I DIDN'T MEAN TO HURT YOUR FEELINGS. I JUST GOT A LITTLE SCARED.

The boy looked at the board, reading it. Miraculously, he seemed to understand it.

I CAN STAY FOR A LITTLE WHILE, BUT I HAVE A FRIEND WAITING IN THIS TEMPLE. PLUS, I NEED AIR.

The boy looked back at her, her bulging, red cheeks and strained expression showing she was indeed low on air. He nodded, signalling her to wait. He bolted to a nearby rock, lifted it up and grabbed a big air bubble trapped underneath it. He held it to her, as if to ask, "Will this help?"

Yuki nodded, happily breathing in the air bubble. The air inside was a little dirty with a sandy aftertaste, but at least it eased her aching just a little. She smiled at him in gratitude.

THANKS. I NEEDED THAT.

He smiled back; happy he had made her happy.

SO…YOU MUCH OF A TALKER? BUT I GUESS NOT, CAUSE IT DOESN'T LOOK LIKE THERE'S ANYONE ELSE HERE.

He opened his mouth wide, showing that he has no tongue. Therefore, he cannot speak at all. He could make small sounds, but no words.

YIKES, THAT SUCKS. SORRY.

The boy shook his head, accepting her apology. He looked at her face deeply, suddenly giving a curious look. Yuki got a little nervous. He reached over to her face, cupping her puffed cheek in his hand. Then he gently squeezed it, making her blush.

"Okaaaaay, this is getting a little weird. But I'll humour him."

As he held her cheek, she blew a bubble or two in response. He quietly laughed, repeating this several times like a child playing with a new toy, making Yuki a little uncomfortable. Yuki could see the juvenile-like joy in this boy's eyes and it made her smile too as she playfully poked his cheek. The boy got closer, now hugging Yuki while nuzzling her now deep red face.

(Very comfortable)
(Not so comfortable)
SQUISH

Yuki was caught off guard, but she knew fighting wouldn't help. So, she hugged back, gently patting his head. The boy then noticed the sapphire necklace around Yuki's neck, entranced by it.

IT'S A PRESENT FROM A FRIEND. SHE GAVE IT TO ME FOR GOOD LUCK.

The boy smiled, kissing the jewel as if he wanted it to be even luckier. That made her giggle behind her cheeks, patting his head as he hugged her closely.

As she looked him over, she noticed the chain that anchored to the ground was locked around his neck. The lock itself had a keyhole at the front. She wrote on her board, tapping his shoulder to get his attention.

YOU'RE A PRISONER HERE?

The boy sadly nodded, weakly rustling with his chain, having long since given up trying to break it.

WHO OR WHAT PUT YOU IN HERE?

The boy looked at Yuki...and pointed behind her towards the hole she was about to escape through.

THERE'S SOMETHING ON THE OTHER SIDE THERE?

The boy nodded again. Yuki then held her hand to her chin, thinking to herself.

"If there's a lock, there must be a key."

She scribbled hastily, thinking of a solution.

THEY LIKELY HAVE THE KEY TO YOUR LOCK. IF I CAN GET IT FROM THEM, I CAN LET YOU OUT OF HERE. AND THEN YOU CAN COME WITH ME.

The boy's eyes widened in horror. He held her tight, shaking his head vigorously as if imploring her not to do that. He then grabbed Yuki's board, scribbling a very rough skull then pointing to her.

YOU'RE SAYING THAT IF I GO, THAT THING COULD…. KILL ME?

Yuki gulped nervously as she wrote that last part. He nodded, confirming her fears. He hugged her again, silently begging for her to stay.

Yuki petted his head, feeling sorry for the poor boy. But she knew what she had to do, for her options were limited. She wrote quickly on her board, hoping he would understand.

I GET YOU'RE SCARED, BUT LET'S BE REAL. IF I STAY HERE, IT'S ONLY A MATTER OF TIME BEFORE YOU RUN OUT OF AIR TO GIVE ME AND I'LL DROWN. BUT IF I LEAVE AND I GET THE KEY, (IF WHATEVER'S WAITING DOESN'T WIPE ME OUT,) I'LL SET YOU FREE AND I'LL BE ABLE TO BREATHE AGAIN.

The boy still didn't want her to leave… but he knew he had to. He loosened his hold on Yuki, letting go as he slowly teared up again. Yuki gently held his shoulders, trying to reassure him.

HEY, DON'T CRY. I'LL BE
BACK. I PROMISE.

Yuki gave him the warmest smile, nuzzling him gently with her cheek. He smiled a little with a light blush as he waved her goodbye, the girl disappeared into the dark passage where the aforementioned danger awaited...

DIVING LOG ENTRY 7

Total time submerged: 60 minutes

Outside the Breathless Temple's gate, Olv waited anxiously, worried for the girl's safety. He ceaselessly twiddled his thumbs, his mind running all over the place. He looked around the temple's features trying to occupy his mind.

"Hmm? What's that at the top?"

Something at the peak of the temple had caught Olv's attention. He glided up to it, leaving the empty air tank back at the entrance. It appeared to be an opening to a hole that extended into the heart of the temple. It was sealed off by a huge, circular, rusted metal weight that only had a few holes big enough to see through.

"Wait...could this be their exit? But that means...."

Olv's eyes widened in horror.

"As long as this weight is here, they're trapped! Well, not on my watch!"

Olv puffed his chest, ready to do his bit to help. There was just one problem...

"How DO I move this blasted contraption out of the way?"

Back inside the temple, Kaia was crawling through a passage of her own, letting out an odd bubble of stale air whenever she needed to. Emerging from the end of the tunnel, she was treated to an unnerving sight: A large stone hall, with what looked like prison cells. It reminded her too much of that prison in Undala Paradiso. That prison would have been her watery grave if not for Olv's royal intervention.

Meanwhile, Yuki was crawling through at a frantic pace, cheeks turning deep blue and set to burst. She let out a large bubble involuntarily every second, moaning in her throat as she was really struggling to hold. Part of her was regretting spending too much time with the strange boy from earlier, but she knew it was the best she could do.

She emerged from the end of the tunnel at full speed, doing a front flip on her way out. Searching around, she saw a very bewildered Kaia and scrambled towards her, pointing to her puckered lips.

"MM! MMM!"

Kaia held her shoulders, writing down at Yuki needed to do.

It's okay. I'll share my air with you. But first you need to let out the stale air. Exhale just a little bit.

Not even questioning it, Yuki exhaled a huge cloud of stale bubbles, freeing up room for Kaia. This made her face turn even darker. Kaia got closer to Yuki...and locked lips with her, making them both red as tomatoes. Kaia exhaled still fresh air into Yuki, relieving pressure in her chest. As she shared her air, Kaia's own chest started to tingle. If she shared too much, she could put herself in danger. She broke away from Yuki, her own face staying red, but relieved that her friend felt better... for now.

Their current air crisis put on hold, the girls searched the area they were in: a huge submerged prison. Looking inside the cells, there were more human remains. They didn't need to say anything. They knew what had happened to these poor people.

Next to one of the skeletons was a note. Kaia reached for it through the bars and read it. They were not ready for what they read:

If you're reading this, then you have a made a terrible error coming here. There is indeed a treasure that grants wishes here. But it is also a death trap. The Guardian protects it mercilessly. It has a weapon that is not of this world. If it doesn't destroy you, it will drag you into this prison... where I am struggling to hold my last breath.

The Guardian is your way out. Your only way out. You need the keystone in its centre to unlock the treasure. As for how... I don't... Air... please...

The rest of the letter is desperate scribbles. Which means whoever wrote it must have run out of time before they could finish it.

This sent a chill down both of their spines, their skin turns a shade paler with fright. The temple was a nightmare, a death trap. They had to get out while they still had breath in their bodies. But not before getting what they came for: the treasure to fix Yuki. Kaia once again clapped her hands in prayer.

Oci Jun,

Mistress of Currents,

Nurse of Reefs,

Take these flooded souls into your warming bosom, So that they

may know peaceful rest in the infinite blue.

With renewed determination and a sense of great care, they clinked their sapphire bracelet and necklace together and pressed on, moving from the prison through a set of massive steel gates that, luckily for them, were already open. But what was on the other side almost made their jaws drop.

They bore witness to the enormous hollow interior of the entire temple, a massive enclosure with dozens upon dozens of ruined pillars, structures and any other form of debris they could think of, great and small.

And somewhere in this massive dwarfing dungeon, where they couldn't even see its end... was the treasure.

Both of their eyes nearly popped out of their heads. Yuki scrambled for her board, not at all okay with this scale.

IS THIS FOR REAL?! HOW ARE WE GOING TO FIND IT IN ALL OF *THIS???*

Kaia scratched her head, racking her brain. She scribbled on her board the best idea she could come up with.

I hate to say it, but it might be best to split up. We'll cover more ground if we split up. If you find something, shine your flashlight straight up. This place is dark enough for them to be seen at a distance.

Do the same if you need air as well. But we'll both need to be quick.

Yuki nodded, holding out her hand for a high five. Kaia responded in kind, their clap echoing through the water. Yuki then remembered something.

WHILE YOU'RE SEARCHING, COULD YOU KEEP AN EYE OUT FOR ANY KEYS? ABOUT THIS BIG?

She extended her fingers indicating a space about half a foot long, to show how big the key should be. Kaia tilted her head in confusion.

Why? Did you find something?

Yuki fidgeted.

WELL, ACTUALLY, *SOMEONE.* A WATER BREATHER LIKE OLV. BUT HE'S LOCKED UP HERE. I PROMISED I'D FREE HIM IF I FOUND THE KEY.

Kaia crossed her arms, highly doubting if they had time for stop overs. But she nodded, agreeing to do it for Yuki with a smile.

Gotcha. I'll keep an eye out.

They split up, going in different directions. Kaia spotted one or two human skeletons right away, thinking they must have been lucky to even get this far.

Every pillar she searched but found only shadows and sand.

Wherever she swam, she found old spears and a couple of odd craters. Some sort of conflict clearly took place here.

Every ruined and destroyed building she explored, she found chests with busted locks and mementos of the past that were ruined by time.

"Ugh, this is going to take forever! And we don't even have that!"

But as far as she knew, she was no closer to finding the treasure.

Yuki found pretty much the same, albeit at a slower pace. The depths of this temple were frustratingly large. They needed a lot of luck to find what they sought...before they both ran out of air.

They searched and searched and searched, the rush almost driving them both nuts.

"No sign of the treasure... or that boy's key."

It took so long, that soon, Yuki needed more air, her face turning red again, her chest heaving. She did what Kaia told her and aimed her flashlight straight up, signalling Kaia to come to her.

On the other side of the expanse, Kaia saw Yuki's light and swam towards it as fast as she could. She swam up higher to get a better view and suddenly in the corner of her eye, she saw something in the darkness.

It looked like a lone spire pedestal that stood in the centre of a marble ring, surrounded with undisturbed sand and untouched stone. That was all she could see in the murky water, but it already looked very promising.

"Right. Change of plan."

Kaia pointed her light towards where the spire was, turning it on again as to signal Yuki to meet her there. Yuki looked on in surprise.

"No way! Did she find something?!"

Yuki paddled as fast as she could, the pressure in her chest growing even worse, her cheeks turning a deep red.

"Mmmng...I can hold it...I can hold it...If Kaia can hold it, I can hold it."

Yuki was thinking to herself over and over, trying to numb the airless burn somehow as she clutched her sapphire necklace. But soon she began to see what Kaia was pointing at, looking at the pristine pedestal, with hopeful eyes.

They regrouped at the rim of the marble ring, sharing air once again to ease Yuki's pressure. She gave a thumbs up and a blush, ready to move on. Kaia couldn't share much more air, as she was starting to feel the strain as well. All the more reason for them both to get a move on.

DIVING LOG ENTRY 8

Total time submerged: 88 minutes

Kaia and Yuki slowly glided towards the pedestal, nervousness in their hearts. They looked upon it...and saw there was a big, diamond shaped groove in the centre of it. They both grimaced in frustration.

Darn, we're missing something. But where the heck do we find it?

Yuki held a hand to her chest, really starting to worry about their chances.

DOESN'T LOOK LIKE HIS KEY, EITHER. GUESS WE'RE BACK TO SQUARE ONE, UNLESS…

Yuki noticed some more worn text beneath the groove. She pointed towards it, showing it to Kaia.

"The treasure lays below this point and your journey's end. But to win this treasure and the day, you must defend an even greater treasure, one that all possess."

They both looked it in puzzlement. Yuki held her chin in thought.

"A treasure we all have, we have to protect to get this treasure? I don't get it..."

But then at that moment, a massive, hostile presence appeared behind the girls, overbearing both of them. A deep, monotone drone echoed as something enormous was coming their way. Neither of them wanted to turn around. But their heads slooooowly rotated...to see a grand machine.

It must have stood at least twenty metres tall, a singular, floating spire with a rotating, red eye at its tip, surrounded by wide, glowing white rings that seemed to emit walls of energy. The entire thing glowed a brilliant white, lighting up the dark, murky cavern round them.

"Whoa...this is like something from one of Yuki's games!" Yuki was not so impressed.

"What. The. Heck. Is. THAT. THING?!"

The machine glared at the frightened girls, its eye pointing a laser at both of them. The rings around it then started to shift and spin, revealing a large glowing object mounted on the top ring... that looked suspiciously like a cannon.

Surely, we're able to talk with this thing, right? Maybe it'll help us get the treasure, if we ask nicely.

The cannon-like object was giving a high-pitched wail as it charged.

NOPE. I DON'T THINK SO. SCATTER!

They darted off in opposite directions before the cannon discharged, sending out a high-powered laser could cut through stone. They both hid behind massive piles of debris as the machine began its hunt. Kaia hyperventilated in her cheeks from sheer fright.

"That was WAY too close! What do we do now?!"

Yuki was thinking the same thing, covering her mouth as her heart raced.

In that frightening moment, both Kaia and Yuki understood what the riddle meant: to reach the treasure, they would have to defend a treasure they both have:

Their lives.

Yuki exhaled a bubble, which caught the machines attention. It made a loud droning sound as it slowly approached Yuki's position. She's curled up in fear, unsure of what to do and whimpered in her throat.

"Yuki!"

Seeing her friend in danger, Kaia swam out into the open to draw its attention. The machine turned towards her with an alarming red light, setting its sights on her. Firing laser after laser, each one missing Kaia by a hair.

Yuki noticed what was going on and fled to another spot, hiding behind a ruined stone pile. She huddled in terror, her heart racing as fast as her scattered mind.

"How did this happen? Why did this happen? Why to me? WHY??"

Yuki was in pure despair, covering her ears from the chaos outside, her chest starting to throb. Opening her eyes just a crack, she could see a ruined lockbox. She crawled towards it, grabbing it with one hand to look inside.

There was a key. A rustproof key, with a familiar tip.

Yuki's eyes lit up with newfound hope.

Meanwhile, Kaia had managed to give the machine the slip for the moment. Letting her body settle to conserve air, she was racking her brain for some idea, ANY idea to help survive against this thing.

She looked at it from a corner, seeing it turn away.

"Now's my chance! Do or die!"

She grabbed a nearby spear from the wreckage swimming behind the machines blind spot, jamming it between two of the machine's uppermost rings. The energy flow was disrupted, making the rings arc and flash chaotically before breaking apart with an explosive flash, leaving its eye wide open.

The machine did not like this.

With a loud mechanical roar, the machine exhaled a violent current, sending Kaia flying out of control, out of range... and out in the open.

The laser charged again, aiming directly at Kaia. There was no time to swim to cover. She was a fish in a barrel.

"OLV!"

She screamed in her mind, certain of what would happen next as she braced herself.

THUD!

A dull crash behind the machine caught its attention, sparing Kaia for the moment. It looked behind, seeing Yuki slowly swimming away.

It aimed its laser, already charged and trained on her. Yuki looked at it in surprise, shielding her eyes.

The laser fired, speeding right towards her...

"YUKIIIIII!"

The laser struck.

Not Yuki herself...

But rather her sapphire necklace. The laser rebounded off the jewel, sending it in a completely different direction. Both Kaia and Yuki saw that...

And they both had a brainwave.

They both scrambled to cover and out of the confused machine's sight, regrouping behind a toppled pillar.

THESE JEWELS ARE PRISMS. THEY CAN REFRACT ANY LIGHT THAT GOES THROUGH THEM. IF MINE CAN DO IT, THEN YOURS CAN TOO.

Kaia looked at her sapphire bracelet, nodding in understanding.

Okay... but how do we use it against that thing?

Yuki gave a big, confident smile.

WE BEAT IT AT ITS OWN GAME.

The machine was still searching for its targets, now more aggressively than ever as it resorted to cutting through cover to find them.

Kaia emerged from the shadows, flashing her light at the machine as if to provoke it.

And provoke it she did. The machine took aim instantly, charging up much quicker now before discharging its deadly payload.

But Kaia smiled at the machine, as if she and Yuki were about to win.

She raised her sapphire bracelet at the last second, but the refracted laser went off course, hitting random debris and scattering dust through the water. She had to try again.

"Blebblh!"

Kaia pulled down her eyelid at the machine, sticking out her tongue as she taunted it. The machine didn't take kindly to that, as it simply charged up another shot.

This time, she was ready.

Raising her bracelet again, the laser rebounded in a new direction, this time towards Yuki, who in turn had raised her sapphire necklace to further refract the laser...right back at it.

The machine's weapon had struck its own eye, shattering it into a million pieces before its entire body came crashing down, lifeless.

All that remained among the wreckage of the machine was a single, faintly glowing diamond, the exact shape of the groove in the pedestal.

The girls got together and gave a celebratory high five into a fist bump, ecstatic in their victory. But their celebration was short lived as both of them exhaled stale air, meaning they were both short on time.

Let's celebrate afterwards.

Yuki nodded, swimming to the pedestal, whilst Kaia grabbed the stone from the machine's carcass and re-joined her. They slotted it in and watched it fit perfectly, the pedestal glowed a bright blue before sinking into the ground. The entire expanse began to shake and rumble immensely, as the floor below them opened, shifting away the ruined landscape they were already familiar with.

And their prize...

A literal sea of golden treasure.

DIVING LOG ENTRY 9

Total Time Submerged: 2 Hours 6 minutes

Kaia and Yuki's eyes lit up gold, utterly gobsmacked by this impossible fortune. They both shook their heads and began to look around, for they were not here for gold. They were here for one thing and one thing alone.

It didn't take them long to find it.

A shining crystal jewel. Shining a brilliant bluish white, it stood out, even among the glimmering gold as it gave it off a magical aura. If it was anything, that would have been the treasure they were seeking. Kaia brought Yuki over to it, nodding to her.

Go on, make your wish, Yuki. Make it count.

Yuki gently lifted the jewel and pressed it against her head, closing her eyes and focusing on what she wanted most of all...

"I want..."

"I wish..."

"I need..."

Yuki was struggling to find the right words. She only had one chance. She couldn't afford to waste it. Kaia patiently waited, her own air growing thin.

Then, in an epiphany, she found the words.

"I wish for me, Kaia and that boy to leave this place and love the ocean again, together!"

She cried out in her head, hoping a thought was enough.

The jewel sheened a blinding white, giving a loud twinkling sound. The jewel's magical aura resonated through the water going in two different directions: one straight up, revealing a door to the surface, and one to a hidden passage, leading back to where Yuki had come from.

Both of them smiled…. Then both let out a huge cloud of air, their faces turning deep blue. They really were out of time. Kaia darted straight up, towards the hatch, towards the surface… but Yuki went back towards the gate, Kaia grabbing her arm.

Where are you going?! The surface is that way!

THERE'S SOMETHING I HAVE TO DO FIRST!

Neither of us have the air to stay any longer, girl!

THEN GO ON AHEAD! I'LL CATCH UP! PLEASE THERE'S NO TIME.

Yuki was right. There really was no time, not even to argue. Kaia reluctantly let her go, swimming upwards, hoping to everything that was holy to her, that Yuki would keep her word. Straight up, she swam, letting out air every second, her cheeks set to burst. She could see a light at the top of the tunnel that was steadily getting bigger, as if something was moving. As she got closer, she saw a weight on the temple that would have blocked her escape, dooming her in this critical moment!

But strangely yet luckily, it was moved just enough for her to fit through. She squeezed her body through, finally free from the temple and back out in the open ocean. Looking around, next to the weight she saw Olv, flat on the stone and exhausted, catching his breath.

"Did he push this thing? Wow, he must be really strong." Kaia

let out more stale air, her chest on fire.

"Urgh, never mind that!"

Kaia shook Olv's shoulders violently, snapping him out of his daze. He looked up in confusion and saw Kaia's strained face right in front of him.

"Kaia, you made it! But goodness, you're like a berry!"

Kaia pointed upwards, letting out more air.

"Right! Hold on tight!"

Olv wrapped his arm around Kaia, swimming straight up whilst carrying her. Kaia covered her mouth and nose, trying to hold it in for just that little bit longer...

Kaia and Olv broke the surface together, the former taking in a huge gasp of much-needed air, colour at last returning to her face. She held her boyfriend as strength returned to her body.

"Kaia, are you all right?"

Kaia lifted her head, smiling at her caring boyfriend.

"Wait a moment. Where's miss Yuki?!"

Kaia looked downwards, fearing for her friend...

Back down in the temple, the boy from earlier was shaken and on alert from all the shaking that was happening, curling up against a stone in fear.

He started to hear something with his sensitive ears. Something approaching. The sound of bubbles, a muffled groan. He looked towards the dark, cramped passage...and saw Yuki emerge from it, a key in her hand. His face lit up with pure joy, free from any past sorrow.

He hugged Yuki as she hastily slotted the key into his neck chain, popping loose with an audible click before dropping to the ground. He gently touched his neck, no longer bound. He felt so incredibly...indescribably happy.

But Yuki tapped him, interrupting his moment of liberation. She hastily scribbled on her board, not even caring for neatness.

I'M GLAD YOU'RE FREE AND I KEPT MY PROMISE, BUT I NEED YOUR HELP BADLY. I'M STRUGGLING TO HOLD MY BREATH AND I NEED TO GET TO THE SURFACE. I

DON'T WANT TO DROWN! PLEASE HELP ME GET UP THERE!

She held the sign to him, pleading in desperation, her face getting bluer by the second. The boy could see she was in pain and nodded, wrapping his arms around her as she clamped her own around her nose and mouth.

The boy took off with her in tow at breakneck speed, gliding through the dark, tight passage with minimal effort, not even bumping any of the walls. He came out of the tunnel like a greyhound out of the track, leaving behind a wake of swishing water and bubbles.

The boy saw the ceiling passage, rocketing straight up into it, rising as fast as he could. Yuki's cheeks were bulging, her face a deep, dark purple. Her vision was growing dark. Her body was growing weak.

"Please...air!"

Seeing the light from the open ocean all around her, she knew she was out of that nightmare of a temple. But as they rose closer and closer to the surface... the last of her strength faded.

"It's too much... I'm done."

Yuki let go. her limbs went limp, her now useless air erupting out in one big, continuous stream as her cheeks slowly deflated and her eyes slowly shut...

Her ears heard the sound of splashing, the muffling water no longer around her face. She took a huge breath by pure instinct, coughing heavily as colour finally returned to her face. Yuki caught her breath, looking up and saw the boy holding her in his arms, a worried expression on his face.

She chuckled weakly, speaking in between ragged breaths.

"Don't worry...I'm...okay now. You really... saved my

butt.... Thanks."

The boy only hugged her, silently crying tears of joy.

"YUKI!!"

Kaia and Olv rushed over to them, the boy giving Olv a unfamiliar stare. Olv did the same, staring in pure bewilderment.

"Impossible...she found...an Abyssal One?!"

Kaia looked at Olv and at the boy.

"What's an Abyssal One?"

Olv broke his shocked gaze, regaining his composure and clearing his throat.

"Ahem, apologies. Abyssal One's are much like my people, humanoids living underwater. But Abyssal One's are far more secretive, choosing to live at the bottom of ocean trenches miles deep, where there's almost no light. They are master hunters, able to outswim just about anything, which is quite fortuitous in Miss Yuki's case."

Yuki only gave a weak thumbs up before her hand limply plopped back into the water.

"Unfortunately, an unknown calamity almost spelled the end for them. No-one knows what actually happened, but it almost wiped them out. This one before us may be among the last of his kind."

Kaia felt bad for the boy, seeing him being locked up in that temple, in addition to his race being driven to the edge of extinction. His eyes were squinted, meaning sunlight was a new experience for him. She paddled up to him, patting his head.

"Thank you for saving my friend. We owe you our lives."

The boy simply smiled with a happy blush.

But then, below them, the temple rumbled deeply, making them uneasy. They all peeked under, looking at the pyramid structure...and a sea of gold erupted from the top and every exit. The once dark and looming Breathless Temple, was now half buried under an impossible amount of gold and treasure, more than enough for just about everyone.

They all looked at each other blankly, not expecting this at all. Olv chose to break the silence.

"...Mmmaybe the temple is rewarding us for besting it?" A

long pause passed between them.

"Yeah, let's go with that."

They all agreed in unison, not even bothering to question it at this point.

"So…"

Kaia held a hand to the back of her head.

"Do we grab some? As a souvenir?" Olv

nodded.

"But only a bagful for each of us. I fear any more would be too cumbersome."

They all agreed to that, Olv passing out a small woven sack for each of them, even the Abyssal One. Yuki finally started treading water under her own strength.

"Fine by me, but someone else can fill up my share. I've held my breath MORE than enough for one day."

Just as she finished that sentence, the Abyssal One had dived, gathered his share and Yuki's and surfaced again, presenting it to her.

"Whoa…you ARE quick. Thanks."

Bewildered, she took the bag, which was not too heavy to weigh her down.

"Well, I got my wish, made a new friend and got some loot. So…do we head back?"

They all nodded in unison.

"Yeah, me too. To heck with this place. Though it's a waterlogged bank now, so it's not so bad."

She then looked at the Abyssal One.

"Wanna come back to our place?"

He smiled happily, nodding without hesitation. He hugged and nuzzled her, making her blush. He then gently poked her cheeks again.

"Not this again...I'm not holding my breath right now, silly!"

Kaia and Olv simply laughed at this exchange.

"Kaia, I firmly believe a beautiful new bond may be forming before us."

Kaia nodded with a genuine grin.

"Yeah, I think these two are going to get along juuuust fine."

As the sun was beginning to set, they raced back to Ark Epsilon before dark, not wanting their parents to catch on to what they had just done.

The next day, their lives, Yuki's in particular, would begin anew. Yuki slept soundly that night... for her wish came true, and the nightmares had stopped.

DIVING LOG ENTRY 10

1 Month since the big dive

A month passed since Kaia and Yuki conquered the Breathless Temple. Kaia and Yuki shared their discoveries with their parents, after they realised Yuki's change in demeanour.

Initially they were shocked and angry that their children had done something so dangerous, but when they saw what they had gained from that risk, they couldn't be help but be thankful, especially to Kaia and Olv.

They gained enormous funds from their findings at the Breathless Temple, keeping its existence a secret from the general public. The funds were then shared between the two families and the higher ups at Ark Epsilon, who used it to improve it to improve the overall quality of life on the artificial island. Whatever wasn't needed was donated to a number of charities.

Yuki's family had also gathered enough funds for a bigger home... a floating home, to be exact, outside the island, right near Kaia's place. The three of them were adjusting quickly to their home...and not long after, they welcomed a fourth member.

Kaia left the house that morning, eager to see Yuki at her new place. She broke out into an excited sprint, pure excitement and joy running through her soul.

30 or so houses down the pier, there it was, Yuki's new home. It was a similarly sized chestnut home, albeit a bit smaller than Kaia's home, but with a different interior layout and one huge difference: There was an elevated hatch on top of a small circular water tank in almost every room, even the kitchen and bathroom, opening to the water below and a small submerged room downstairs. This was an accommodation for the Ruki family's fourth resident.

"Yo, Yuki! It's Kaia."

Kaia knocked at the front door, waiting for permission to be let in. Yuki's father, more chipper than before, greeted Kaia with a wave.

"Oh, hello Kaia! You must be here for Yuki?"

Kaia nodded, looking around the crisp, new enclosure, the smell of new furniture and sea salt mixing together.

"She is in her room. Right at the end of that hall, just like before. Her new boyfriend is here too."

She bowed in gratitude, before slowly walking down the hall, knocking on Yuki's door.

"Come in!"

Kaia entered, seeing Yuki's new room for the first time. It was bigger than before, with a huge glass window facing the open ocean, her single bed, a bigger desk for her computers and gaming consoles, a bigger in-wall wardrobe and shelves for storage and of course, the same ocean hatch as in every room.

Yuki was sitting in her wheelchair, working on her computer, furiously typing away. Next to her was the Abyssal One she had found in the temple, resting his arms and chin on the edge of the hatch, watching Yuki with quiet awe.

"Hey there, buddy! Been a while since I saw you!"

Kaia patted the One's head, making him give a catlike grin in enjoyment. Yuki turned to her with a happy look and a blush.

"I named him a while ago. His name is Octo. We're also… kinda dating now. He always cuddled every time we met, so I thought, why not spend more time together…and maybe get closer?"

Yuki wheeled over to Octo, scratching his chin gently. He gently holds her hand, nuzzling it lovingly.

"See? He can't get enough of me. He even sometimes drags me down to his room and cuddles with me like crazy until I need air."

Octo nods and holds her other hand, gently tugging her with puppy dog eyes.

"Not now, sweetie. Maybe after dinner, ok?" He

pouted and rested his chin. Kaia laughed.

"That's so me and Olv, it's too funny!"

She then noticed the computer screen, displaying a map template and what looked like a sheet of programming code.

"What'cha working on, Yuki?"

Yuki looked back at her screen, eager to show her.

"My first, real project. It's a new game I wanna publish one day. The goal is simple, get from start to finish in one single breath."

Kaia looked at the template, seeing what looked like an 8-bit tanned girl in a wetsuit as the main character. There was also coding for a male variant of the same description, for those who wished for it.

"They look a lot like me."

Yuki nodded.

"That's because you're the model behind them. You inspired me, Kaia."

Kaia scratched the back of her head, laughing sheepishly with a blush.

"I even came up with a name for the game. It's called…" *One Breath.*"

Kaia gave a huge grin.

"I like it! I like it a lot!"

Yuki giggled, eager to finish it as soon as she could.

"It might take a year or two to finish, but no rush. Plus, I have my Abyssal Boy to keep me company and cheer me on, so it's not all bad."

Octo then stretched and extended his tentacle-like fingers to her face, cupping her cheek softly as she nuzzled it in return. Kaia stared blankly at Octo's fingers.

"...Didn't know he could do that."

Kaia shook her head, reaching into her side pack.

"Anyway, I've been working on a little something myself. Ta-da!"

Kaia pulled out a poster, showing off a well-detailed drawing of Kaia and Yuki underwater, reaching their hands out towards the viewer. The text on the poster read:

"The Young and Bubbly Club! A new underwater social group dedicated to those who love the ocean and everything in it! Free-diving or scuba are welcome, with backup air tanks for safety!

Come talk to Yuki Ruki or Kaia Cayden if you want to take the plunge!"

Yuki was taken aback at this news.

"Whoa...so we're really doing this club thing, huh?" Kaia

nodded with an excited grin, barely able to sit still.

"I mean, it took a little convincing on my parents and the authorities end, plus there was some paperwork stuff to fill out, but yeah, it's all ready to go and I'm SO EXCITEEEED!"

Yuki couldn't help but smile back. This had made her day.

"Are Olv and Octo coming too?"

Kaia nodded eagerly, Octo splashing a little in excitement.

"Sweet! When and where do we start?"

Kaia gave a catlike smile and pulled out a map.

"There's a little sunken boat we can use just a 2-minute swim away from the island, there's no doors or cave-ins or any sorts of trapping hazards, so its safe as safe can be. Our first meeting is tomorrow at 11am. Everything's all set up, all we gotta do is get ready."

Yuki giggled, getting hyped up herself.

"Sweet. Let's do this, buddy!"

The next day, at 10:50 am, Kaia and Yuki waited on a little hire boat beside the pier, Olv and Octo waiting beside them in the water.

"Olv, Octo, you guys set up the backup air tanks and stuff and get ready to surprise them. We'll bring the new club members in."

The two boys nodded, swimming off to the meeting site at breakneck speed. Silently the girls waited, wondering if anyone was going to show up, or if this was a bit too far-fetched. They waited and waited.

Right on time, their patience was rewarded. They were greeted by two young teenagers, both around the same age as Kaia and Yuki. The first of the two was a nervous, dark-skinned boy with dark curly hair, dressed in a full-body wetsuit and a scuba tank on his back.

"Um...this is the underwater club thing, right? I-I'm Joey. My friend Mary wanted me to come along."

Mary being the pink-wetsuit girl next to him. She had flowy light red hair, her face dotted with freckles and circle-rimmed glasses. She gave an excited, goofy grin.

"Aww, shucks, Joey. Aren't you excited too? I sure as heck am!"

She spoke in a happy Southern accent, wrapping her arm around the timid Joey's shoulder and making him blush. Kaia giggled cheekily.

"Well, welcome to the club, you two! I'm Kaia and this is Yuki! We'll take you to the boat shortly."

There were no other arrivals that morning, but they were happy regardless. Their little boat puttering away towards the new club site, Joey was getting a little nervous, Mary trying to comfort him.

"It's alright, Joe-Joe. You got a scuba tank with ya, while I'm the one holdin' my little breath down there. It's got me nervous too."

Joey gulped.

"That's what kinda worries me. What if something happens and you run out of breath?"

Kaia sighed and smiled, speaking to reassure them.

"Don't worry, you two. We've taken every precaution we can. We even extra emergency air tanks ready and...some special guests."

The mention of guests peaked the two's curiosity, making their minds wonder. Yuki turned off the engine, slowing the boat to a halt before dropping the anchor.

"Alright, we're here! Just follow us and dive straight down! Ready?"

They both nodded, Mary taking some deep breaths while Joey checked his tank, quietly admiring his friend's bravery. After one last deep breath in unison, they all dropped into the water, Kaia and Yuki leading them straight down into a small, sunken tugboat with a thick coat of algae on the outside and the hull.

Gliding inside through an open doorway, they each took their seats, Mary spotted a backup air tank and sat it next to her for when she needs it, her cheeks puffed up with a hint of red. Joey sat next to Mary, the hiss from his air tank followed by the sound of exhaled air bubbles filled the silent room.

Kaia and Yuki took turns scribbling on their boards.

Welcome to the Young and Bubbly Club, a new underwater social group for those who love the water and everything in it. You two are our first members.

AND TO KICK THINGS OFF, WE HAVE A LITTLE TREAT FOR YOU. WE'D LIKE TO INTRODUCE OUR BUBBLY BOYFRIENDS!

From the shadows of the boat, Olv appeared from next to Joey and Octo from next to Mary, giving them quite a spook.

"Greetings! I am Prince Olv Atlon, a Gilled One and Prince of Undala Paradiso. And this is Octo, one of the rare Abyssal Ones. Though I should note that he is mute, for future advisement.

The two humans shyly waved to the two water breathers, clearly not expecting this. The two boys took a seat next to their respective girlfriends, Octo nuzzling Yuki's cheek as Kaia wrote.

Olv and I met on a dangerous dive down to the Dark Catacombs, which were the darkest depths of the Sunken Mazes. I almost drowned down there, but Olv saved my life and we've been together since, one year later.

Olv blushed at Kaia's praise, fidgeting in his seat.

Yuki wrote:

I MET OCTO ABOUT A MONTH AGO. I LOST MY LEGS FROM A SHARK ATTACK A LONG TIME AGO, THE LINGERING TRAUMA WAS GIVING ME NIGHTMARES. TERRIBLE NIGHTMARES AND A GENUINE DREAD OF THE WATER. BUT KAIA AND OLV SAVED ME. THEY HELPED ME CURE MY FEAR AND I GAINED A BOYFRIEND WHO HUGS ME EVERY SINGLE DAY.

I USED TO BE AFRAID OF THE WATER. NOW, MUCH LIKE KAIA, I DON'T WANT TO LEAVE IT.

The newcomers cooed at these amazing stories in awe, admiring these two girls and their amazing bravery. Mary's face was turning red, so she took a puff of air from the adjacent tank.

Afterwards, we talked and decided to make our own club for those who share the same passion for the deep blue as we do.

BUT ENOUGH ABOUT US. MARY AND JOEY, OUR NEW CLUB MEMBERS…

Kaia and Yuki raised their boards at the same time.

What's your story?

WHAT'S YOUR STORY?

www.ingramcontent.com/pod-product-compliance
Lightning Source LLC
Chambersburg PA
CBHW071536100726
47908CB00004B/1409